Under the Christmas Tree

For Walter, Armida, and the Roeder clan,
who understand the meaning of Christmas
—N.G.

For my mother, Emily; for my wife, Keava;
and my little girls, Amel and Aya. I love you.
And to my old neighbor Shellie, who helped give my
family our most memorable Christmas ever! Thank you!
—K.N.

Under the Christmas Tree
Text copyright © 2002 by Nikki Grimes
Illustrations copyright © 2002 by Kadir Nelson
Printed in Hong Kong. All rights reserved. www.harperchildrens.com

Library of Congress Cataloging-in-Publication Data
Grimes, Nikki. Under the Christmas tree / by Nikki Grimes ;
illustrated by Kadir Nelson. p.   cm. ISBN 0-688-15999-0 — ISBN 0-688-16000-X
(lib. bdg.) 1. Christmas—Juvenile poetry.   2. Children's poetry, American.
[1. Christmas—Poetry.   2. American poetry.]   I. Nelson, Kadir, ill.   II. Title.
PS3557.R489982 U54   2002   2001024330   811'.54—dc21

Typography by Elynn Cohen 1 2 3 4 5 6 7 8 9 10 ❖ First Edition

Under the Christmas Tree

By Nikki Grimes

Illustrated by Kadir Nelson

HarperCollinsPublishers

The Box

I count down
The days of December
And watch for
The cardboard box
Mom keeps
Like a secret
At the back
Of the closet
All year.
Then, one morning,
It appears
Sudden as fog
And out comes
Three strands of bulbs
Waiting to wink
And imitate starlight,
Leftover tinsel
Still showing off
Its sparkle,
And a basket
Of silver balls
Too delicate
For bouncing.
Magic as mirrors,
They play catch
With every light

In the room.
I dig further and find
The gold acorns
I spray-painted
Last year, a pair
Of quilted reindeer,
And the five-pointed star
Grandma made of lace.
The box bursts with
Forgotten treasures.
But I know we're
Near the bottom
When I find
Jesus, Mary, Joseph,
And the Wise Men,
Their porcelain bodies
Wrapped like mummies.
Do they wonder
Where they've been?
I shrug, then tear their
Tissue-paper shrouds
So they can breathe.
It's then
The Wise Men whisper
Finally
Christmastime is here!

Angel

The angel smiles
Atop the tree
And proves me right.

She's happiest there
Poised for flight.
Halo kissing the ceiling
Feeling closer to home.

Plugged In

Forget the house next door.
What are you waiting for?

    Like precious jewelry
    We stud the rooftop
    Bracelet the porch post
    Bead the bushes
    Pearl the footpath
    And ring the old oak tree.

We are ready and set
To shimmer, so
        Plug
        Us
        In.

Christmas Window

My baby brother's such a child
Squealing, "Mommy! Look!"
Pointing to a store window with
Characters from a book.

The mannequins seem real to him
But I know they're just fake.
Their rosy cheeks are painted on.
Their pearly teeth can't ache.

They're only dolls the store dressed up
To help sell toys and clothes.
I'm six now, so you can't fool—hey!
Did one just scratch his nose?

Jingle Bells

Little ears hear
What others don't
Like sleep-hungry Mai-Ling
Who notices a shy tinkling
And cries, "Mommy, listen."
So Mommy hears

> Cathedral chimes
> Trains thundering underground
> Homeward-bound stomping feet
> And city buses wheezing
> Down the street.

But Mai-Ling hears
A self-conscious *ping*
A bell that softly sings

> Please Give
> Please. Give.
> Please.

Lullaby

On the avenue,
Street vendors
Stomping out the cold
In booted feet
Compete for attention
Hawking chestnuts
And cheap toys.
"Only four more
Shopping days
Till Christmas!"
They remind anyone
Who'll listen.
But yesterday
It was Rhythm Brown
The blind sax-man
Who drew a crowd.
He leaned into
His horn and blew
"Silent Night"
As if he heard
The Baby's cry
And longed to soothe
And swaddle Him
In melody
Soft as a sigh.

Dreaming

Just wait.
Next year
I'll be back
At this rink
But not to drink
Hot chocolate
Or warm a seat
On the sidelines.
This time,
I'll have blades
On my feet.
The night'll be windy
The way it is now.
A fir tree
Exactly like this one
Will bow and shiver
In the plaza
Showing off

Her gown of lights,
And harried shoppers
Will stop and stare
At *me*
Gliding across
The square.
I'll do a sit-spin
On the ice,
Etch a fancy
Figure eight,
Toss in
A triple-flip
Land it clean—
Me! Jolene!
You watch!
I'll skate
I'll float
I'll fly.

Treasure Hunt

It's not in Dad's closet
Or stowed on his shelf.
It's not in Mom's dresser.
I've searched there myself.
It's not in the dryer,
The washer, the fridge,
Nor tucked in the toy chest
Or baby's carriage.
It's not in the foyer
(Sis calls it "the hall")—
And don't tell me Santa
Left nothing at all!
I'm certain to find it.
Mind you, I'm a whiz.
My gift is here somewhere—
Whatever it is!

Smart Art

My mother's gift
Hides inside
An old shoebox.
But who's to tell?
My clever fingers
Veil the drab container
With silvery paper
And ruby ribbon
While just outside
Snowflakes
Erase the world.

Still Life

Sparkling white, hushed in velvet—
Even the city, herself, is in shock.

Wings

The intersection—
Giggling angels leave their prints
In fresh fallen snow.

All I Need

Friends, an icy patch,
A trash-can lid, and speed is
All the fun I need.

House Calls

He totes

His shopping bag

Of goodies

House to house.

I tag along

Giggling

And greedy for

The look of surprise

In the eyes of aunt,

Cousin, uncle, friend.

Merry Christmas!

He intones

Leaving off the

Ho, ho, ho!

And never mind

The chimney

Or the sleigh.

He prefers

The front door

And his black MG.

But Dad still thinks

He's Santa.

Mistletoe

Come to Aunt Joetta's
Christmas party
And a whiff of spiced cider
Mixed with pine
Is not the only thing
That'll greet you
At the door.
Before you can
Use your mouth
For speaking,
Aunt Joetta covers it
With a kiss,
And hugs you
Like a mother bear
Minus the claws. Then
It's Uncle Moe's turn
To squeeze the life
Out of you
But not before
He gives Aunt Joetta

A peck on the cheek
As if he wants
To get in
A little practice
For New Year's.
By the time
You've made it past
All the relatives
Your poor face
Is tattooed
With lipstick.
Call me crazy
But I don't understand
Why Aunt Joetta
Started hanging mistletoe
This year
When it's clear
Nobody in this family
Is desperate
For a reason
To kiss.

Christmas Eve

We join the carolers Jingle-
Belling down the street,
My mom and me.
"Joy to the World"
And everyone we see
Along Columbus Avenue.
We gain a few sopranos
At Mt. Zion where
We polish the Eve
With candlelight.
"We Three Kings of Orient Are"
There to greet us as we
Slide into the pews.
The lights grow dim.
I prick my ears
And listen for the hymn
"O Little Town of Bethlehem."
I scarcely breathe
Afraid to break the spell.
"O Come, O Come, Emmanuel."
The ushers pass candles
Down each pew.

"Hark! The Herald Angels Sing"
And so do we, while first
One candle is lit
Then two, then three.
"Away in a Manger."
Two-handed, I manage
To hold my candle still,
My heart thundering until
The flame is finally
Passed to me.
"Angels We Have Heard on High."
Imagining the candle
Is a straw
I sip its glow
And bow my head to hear
The story we all know.
Then, once dismissed
The crowd and I
Parade into the night
Slightly giddy
And primed
For miracles.

Under the Tree

Under the tree
Something's glowing
And I find my
Interest growing.

Is it tinsel?
Is it foil?
What's that smell
Of perfumed oil?

Can't be myrrh
And frankincense.
What is it?
I hate suspense.

Why'd the presents
Disappear?
What's that cradle
Doing here?

What's that mooing,
Braying sound?
Why's there hay
Spread on the ground?

What's that licking
Up my face?
It's my Labrador
Named Chase.

There's no tree
I'm still in bed.
I rub my eyes
And shake my head

Then run downstairs
To check the tree—
There's that glow!
Can others see?

Getting to the Good Stuff

I love to open presents
On Christmas Eve, at night.
I love to guess the contents
Then see if I was right.

I love the bits of ribbon
The way the endings curl.
I love the dainty wrapping—
Just perfect for a girl.

I love the tissue paper
That teases "almost there!"
So what if I'm now eighty-three?
Go right ahead and laugh at me
And see how much I care!

Private Conversation

Just between us,
Feel free
To keep the lights
Angel hair
Silver bells
Pint-size Santas
And the star.
But listen, Tree,
The popcorn
And the candy canes—
Those belong to me.

Going Nuts

Grandma set out food to munch:
Cashews, walnuts, buttercrunch

Olives, pickles (sour and sweet)
Pickled herring (there's a treat!)

Then she served up holiday fare
On her Christmas chinaware:

Turkey, yams, and mustard greens
Oyster stuffing, French string beans

Cranberry jelly, gravy, bread.
"I'll just have a taste," I said.

Then I piled my plate up high,
But saved a space for pecan pie.

Baby Jesus

Christmas—His cradle
Is empty. Did He grow up?
Is He Santa now?

Neighborhood Santa

Santa—the tan one
On the corner, does he live
At the North Pole, too?

Sad Good-bye

Each year, I put it off.
My mother, patient, waits.
"It's time," she whispers
Nudging me toward
The broom closet.
I grab the ugly tool
With unhappy hands
Gather the pine needles
In a brittle pile
And sweep Christmas
Out the door.

Special Visitors

One kissed my forehead
When he thought I was sleeping.
Yes! There are angels.